Look up into the sky. Can you see the rainbow? It arches like a bridge over the hills and comes down into Nutshell Wood. At the end of the rainbow, deep in the wood, a tiny magical village is appearing. That village is Rainbow's End. Rainbow's End can only be seen by humans when a rainbow is in the sky, otherwise it is invisible to everyone except the gnomes who live there and the woodland animals.

The gnomes of Rainbow's End are jolly little folk who are always busy. Lots of exciting and interesting things happen in the village and no one is ever bored. This book tells the story of something that happened there. A little bird told me!

Rainbow's End

The Winter Warming
Written by Jane Patience
Illustrated by John Patience

PUBLISHED BY PETER HADDOCK LIMITED
BRIDLINGTON, ENGLAND

© Rainbow's End Productions

One fresh Spring morning Dewy Hornbeam and his daughter Hazel were out as usual, gathering ladles of dew from the wild woodland flowers. Although Winter now seemed far away, they were already preparing for the Winter Warming Feast, which took place every year on Egg Hill in Rainbow's End. The Winter Warming was a bright spot in the midwinter when the days were short and the nights long and dark. Everyone looked forward to it with great excitement, especially the children.

The Summer had gone by and now Winter was really here. In the cellar of Hornbeam House, Dewy and his wife, Posy, surveyed their stock of barrels. There were many different kinds of dew, each named after the flower it had been gathered from, and each with its own distinctive flavour. "Well, Posy," said Dewy. "Which three shall we take this year?" "It is such a difficult choice," Posy replied. "The May Bluebell dew was especially nice this year, but then the April Primrose was very good, too."

Posy and Dewy decided to take the May Bluebell, April Primrose and July Campion dews to the Winter Warming. Dewy loaded up the cart while Hazel harnessed their hedgehog, whose name was Parsley, since this herb was her favourite food. This was a tricky job because Parsley's spikes got in the way, but she was a very patient and gentle creature and stood quietly while Hazel put on her bridle. Then they were off. Although the Feast wasn't until the next evening, Dewy always delivered the barrels a day early to allow the dew inside to settle after the bumpy cart ride.

As the cart went along the track, one of the wheels came loose and the cart fell on to one side, with an awful CRASH. The barrels of dew rolled off the cart and down the steep hill with a dreadful rumbling sound, like thunder! Some of them splashed into the stream and sunk out of sight, but the barrel of April Primrose went crashing through the door of the bakery, where Flap Jack, the baker, was putting the finishing touches to the acorn bread for the Feast. ''Oh no!'' he cried. ''My bread's all ruined and there are no more acorns left in the Town's stores.''

As Dewy and Hazel stood by the stream, wondering how they could retrieve the sunken barrels, they heard a 'plopping' sound and saw the small head of an otter bob up out of the water. "Don't look so glum," the otter said. "I'll get my friends to help and we'll have your barrels on dry land in no time." Hazel was sent to fetch a rope from the cart and when she returned she was accompanied by Bristly Oaksbeard, the blacksmith, who had come to lend a hand. The otters dived down to the bottom of the stream and tied one end of the rope around one of the barrels. Then the gnomes pulled it up on to the bank. Soon all the barrels had been rescued. ''Thank you for your help,'' Dewy said to the otters. ''I only wish there was some way of replacing the acorn bread, too.'' None of them noticed the little face that peered down at them from the branches of a nearby tree.

Later that afternoon a chattering procession of squirrels came scampering into Town, each carrying a few acorns wrapped in a tiny leaf bag. "We have brought you these acorns from our own Winter stores," said their leader. "We heard of your accident this morning and would not like the gnome folk to be without acorn bread at their Feast of the Winter Warming."

All through the night, Dusty Miller worked hard to grind the acorns into flour in his windmill. Down at the bakery the next morning, Flap Jack made the flour into lots of tiny loaves of sweet-smelling acorn bread, ready for the Feast that evening.